zolocolor!™

DOODLING BETWEEN BLACK AND WHITE

designed and illustrated by
byron glaser & sandra higashi

LITTLE SIMON

New York London Toronto Sydney

color affects every part of our lives in ways that we often take for granted. Red can make us stop. Or it can stimulate our appetite. Green can make us go. Or it can soothe and calm us.

somewhere between black and white

lies an infinite range of hues, tones, patterns, textures, moods and ideas that make up the colorful spectrum of your imagination. This book is designed to spark your creativity and inspire the many uncommon ways to color. Feel free to color inside, outside, on, and around the lines. Color on the black or not. Make up your own shapes within the shapes. Let your imagination lead you. Use one or many art media: color pencils, felt-tip markers, crayon, or chalk. Explore the limitations, then go beyond. The sky's the limit! And not necessarily blue. The important thing is that you have fun and make it your own. Just color!

LITTLE SIMON

An imprint of Simon & Schuster Children's Publishing Division

New York London Toronto Sydney

1230 Avenue of the Americas, New York, New York 10020

Copyright © 2011 by Zolo Inc. All rights reserved, including the right of reproduction in whole or
in part in any form. Zolo®, Zolocolor™, and all related shapes, patterns, and characters are registered
trademarks and properties of Zolo Inc., Fredericksburg VA 22401 USA www.zolo.com
LITTLE SIMON is a registered trademark of Simon & Schuster, Inc., and associated colophon
is a trademark of Simon & Schuster, Inc. For information about special discounts for bulk purchases, please
contact Simon & Schuster Special Sales at 1-866-506-1949 or business@simonandschuster.com.
The Simon & Schuster Speakers Bureau can bring authors to your live event. For more information or to
book an event contact the Simon & Schuster Speakers Bureau at 1-866-248-3049 or visit our website at
www.simonspeakers.com.

Manufactured in China 0611 SCP

First Edition

2 4 6 8 10 9 7 5 3 1

ISBN 978-1-4424-2261-2

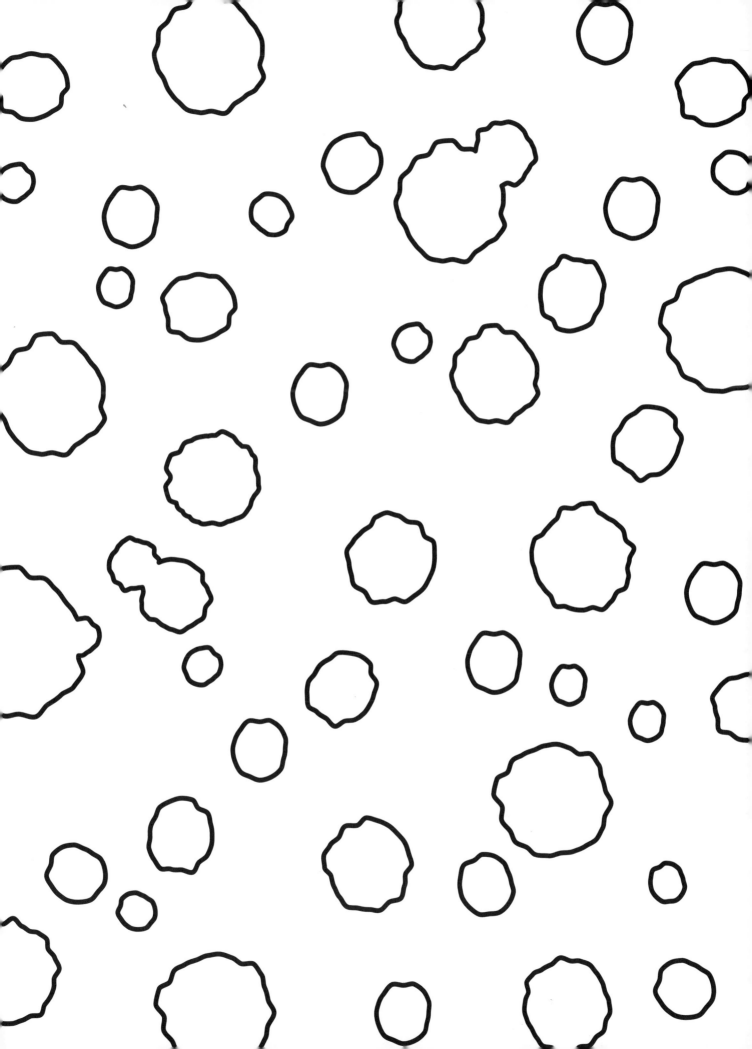

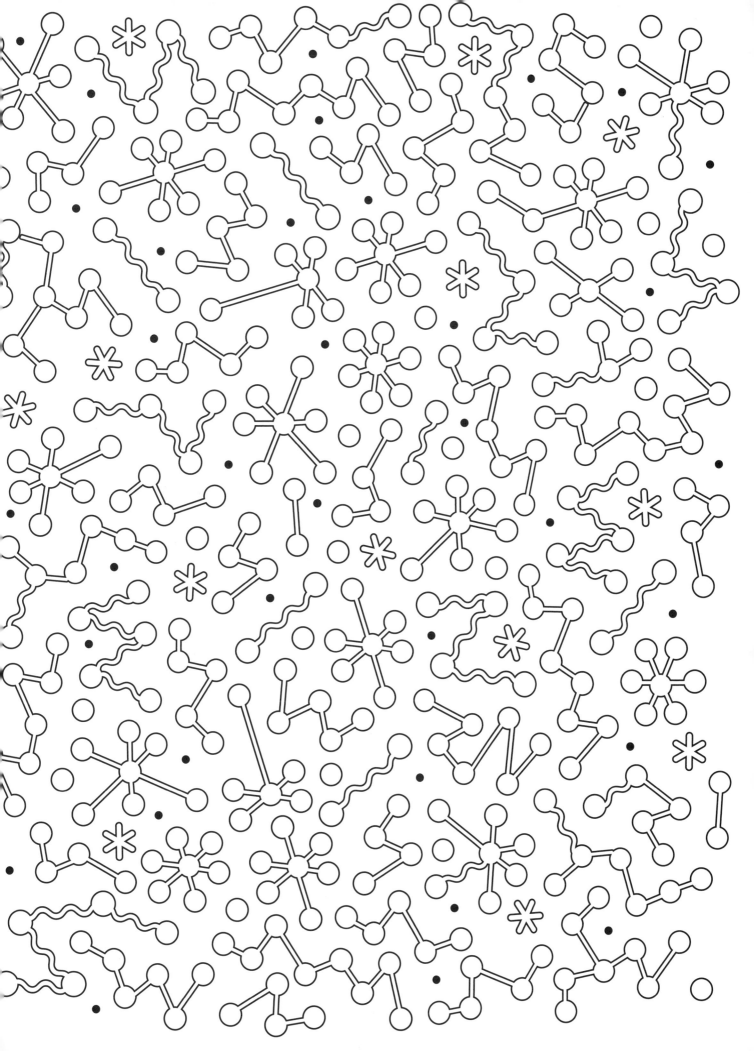

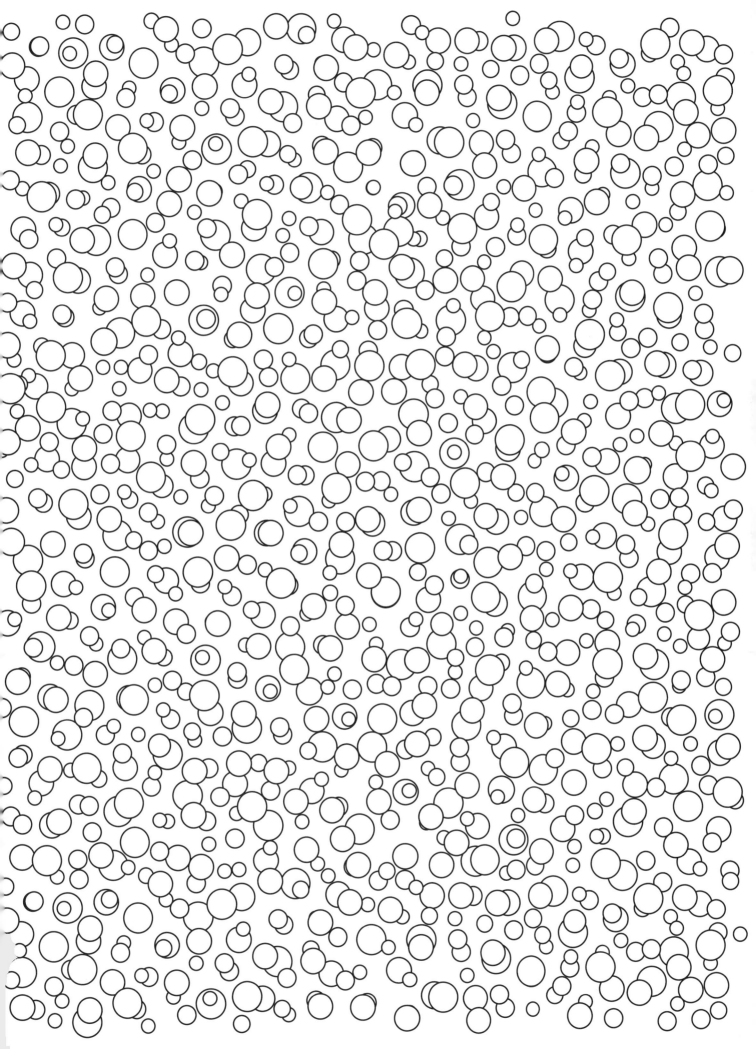

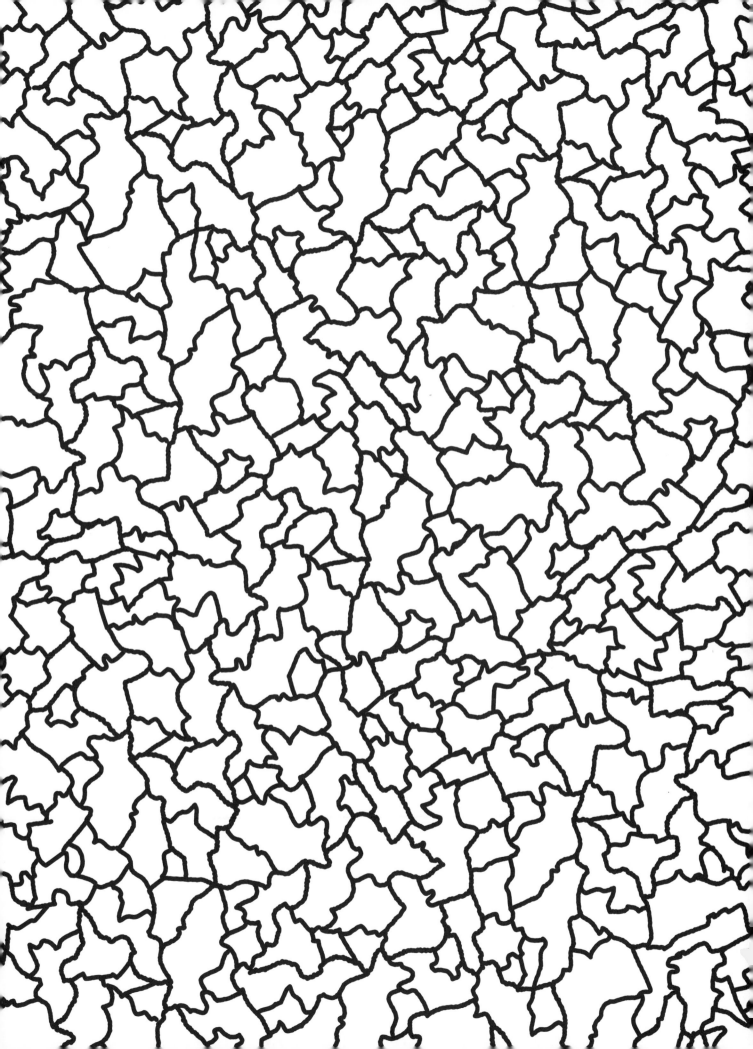

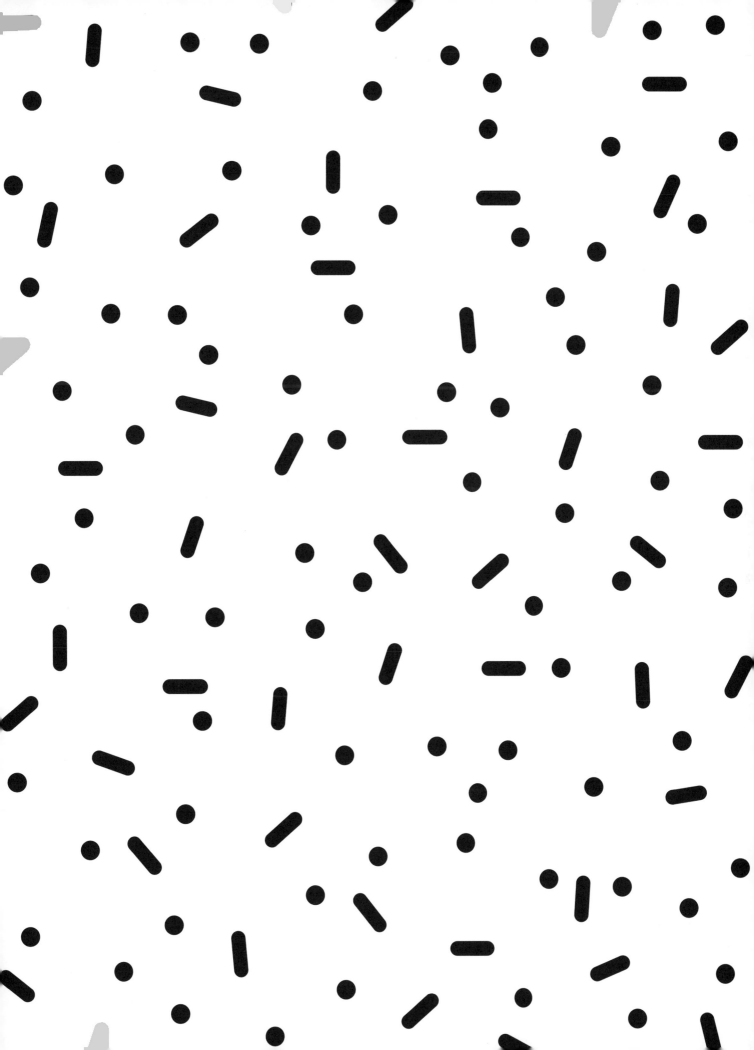

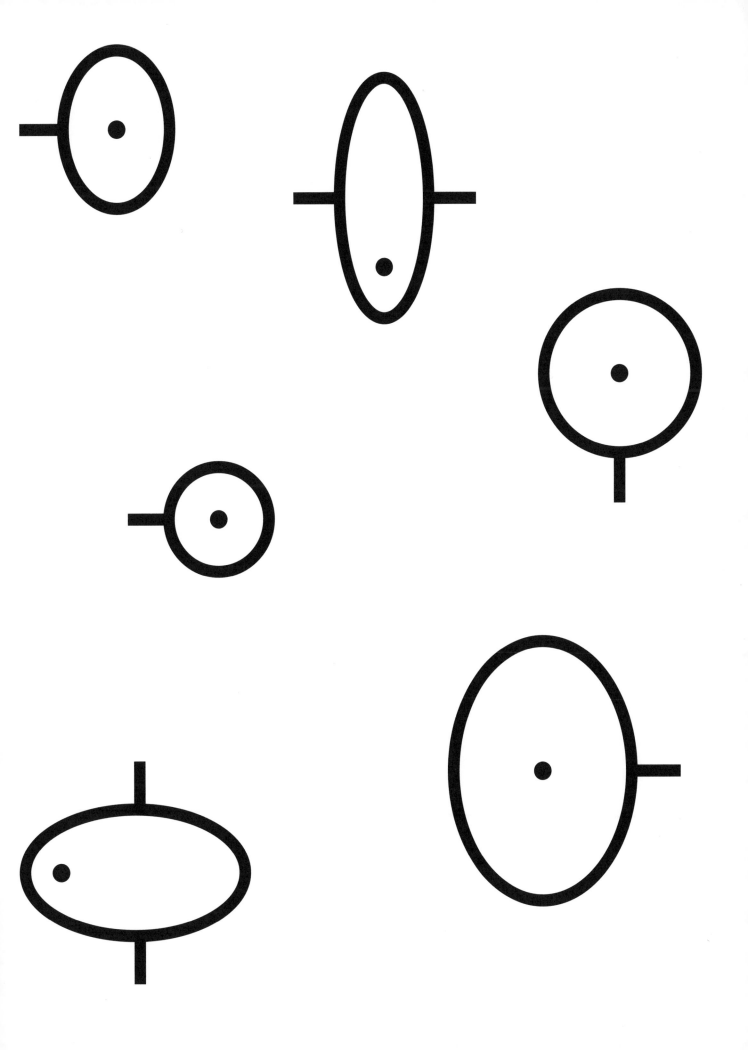

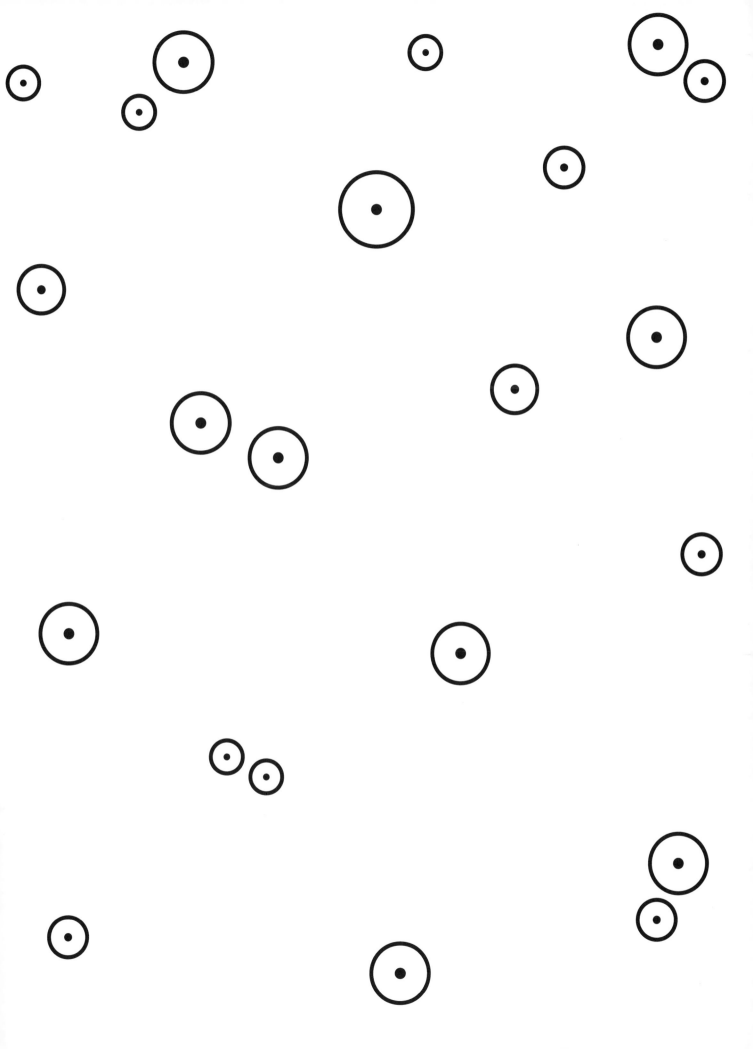